SCHOOL TIMES

AN UNUSUAL ASSEMBLY

(for St Mary's Primary School, Ashford)
RS

No way can they pin this on me!
They can't blame me at all.
The dislodged dust
falling from the rafters like snow
glittering in the rays of sunshine
The shrieks, the squeals, the hubbub, the noise...
Paul, bursting into tears
because it's all too much
The yelling and confusion
But for once, it's not me!
I didn't let the pigeon into the hall.

NAMES

SW

Troublemaker
Window-Breaker

Oh, I've been called the lot.

Shoplifter
Thief, Drifter

Names for things I'm not.

Hoodlum, Punk
Head-Full-of-Junk

Why do they think that they...

Chump, Cheat
Belongs-on-the-Street

... deserve the final say?

BEST FRIEND

RS

Usually she sees me from across the playground
And rushes over
All talk and excitement
Like Auntie Rachel's puppy
Usually we swap lunchboxes
I love her dad's cheese and pickle sandwiches
She loves my mum's egg and salad cream
Usually we sit together on the mat
While Miss Moss tells us what's in store
And we listen to the morning poem
And catch up on the continuing exploits of Class Four
But not today
Perhaps she's feeling under the weather
(Dad says this forever rain is getting everyone down)
Perhaps she got out of the wrong side of bed
Perhaps she's anxious about this afternoon's spelling test
Perhaps...
It was something that I said

UNHAPPY HYDRA

SW

Heads, I've got too many.
Family, friends? Not any.
Almost clicked with Hercules.
Big Guy and I were meant-to-bes.
Moment when I turned my back,
Herc the Jerk switched sides and — THWAK!
Thought that we were buds, but no...

Took two weeks for my heads to regrow.

THE TWINS

RS

Look,
Here comes Luke
And Luke's brother, Mike
Although they're twins
Mike looks nothing like Luke
But, strangely, Luke has a look-alike
And stranger still
The look-alike is also called Luke
But Mike has no look-alike, unlike Luke

They call twin Luke, Luke One
And the other Luke, Luke Two
Everyone likes Luke One
And they like Luke's look-alike Luke Two, too
And they like Mike
Who, in many ways, is not unlike his twin
They just don't look alike
Mike lent me his bike.
What's not to like?

WENDELL McRANDAL

SW

Wendell McRandal caused quite a school scandal
By cribbing off Lib Lester's test.
And I heard him mention he earned a detention
When he copped to the crime and confessed.

I note with revulsion he merits expulsion,
But with Wendell no charge seems to stick.
Put nothing above him; the teachers all love him.
That snake makes me physically sick.

IT WASN'T MY FAULT

RS

It wasn't my fault, Mr Walton
That Sammy the Rat ran away
Billy said Miss had told Kenny
That rats always sleep through the day
It wasn't my fault, Mr Walton
He was quick, well, he didn't half go!
But Billy said Miss had told Kenny
That white rats, like Sammy, are slow
It wasn't my fault, Mr Walton
That the rat ran into the canteen
And the cook, Mrs Spratt,
   has a thing about rats
I've never heard such a loud scream!
And it wasn't my fault, Mr Walton
That it caught Mrs Spratt by surprise
And she dropped the hot tray
   she was carrying
And it covered the floor with
   French fries
It wasn't my fault, Mr Walton
I didn't know it would do any harm

And the Head, Mrs Kipper, slipped up on a chip

And crashed into the fire alarm

Billy said Miss had told Kenny

Fire practice was due anyway

So when the whole school trooped out

    to the playground

It was quite a good thing in a way

It wasn't my fault, Mr Walton

From the school cat's point of view it was great

And I know that a rat is expensive to buy

So next time shall we get a class snake?

BACK ROOM BOY

RS

I wrote the poem that Tommy read
In assembly today
I volunteered to be the one
Who puts the paints away

I am the playtime monitor
I take Miss Moss her tea
If someone's needed for a job
Then that someone is me

I passed the ball to Sarah
And Sarah scored the goal
I rehearsed the play with Tina
Prepared her for the role

I like to work behind the scenes
Not in the spotlight's glare
But I thought I'd write this poem
To remind you I am there

ALL MY TEACHERS
ARE MONSTERS

SW

If there's one rule I'll never break,
It's *Don't Be Late for Mrs Krake.*
She won't get cross, but rumours tell
She ate a kid who missed the bell.
She loves the punctual, lauds the prompt,
And those who dawdle end up chomped.

But worse by far than Krakie's wrath
Is Mr Boyle, who teaches Math.
As he's adding fractions at the board,
His Eye, that evil overlord,
Fixes you with vision strange.
It's best to sit well out of range.

And last of all, there's Miss O'Grine,
Who's taught since Nineteen Thirty-Nine,
A teacher, or perhaps... a witch?
But something tells me not to snitch
To Mr Black, our principal...
'Cos I am not invincible.

TEACHER

RS

She's big and wide but moves just like a cat
    along a wall. She smiles like the queen
Her choice of clothes is black
She wears a hat, although occasionally
    she will wear green
She always marks your book in pencil, never pen
Her voice is quiet, as quiet as falling snow
She very rarely rages
Now and again her voice is raised. But does
    she shout? Oh no
She fixes you with eyes as pale as snake
She stops you dead. She sees into
    your soul
You cannot move. Your heart beats
    and you shake
You want to shout, 'I'm sorry.
    Let me go!'
Her class will tell you that
    she's kind and fair
They never misbehave
    They wouldn't dare

WE'RE GOING TO WIN THE SOCCER CUP

RS

You can't blame me
For losing the match
The other ten players
Just weren't up to scratch
I just missed the penalty
The goalie held his nerve
My shot was on target
But the wind made it swerve
I would have come to training
But I didn't feel right
I was playing on my games console
Late into the night
And you know that sleep's important
If we want to win the cup
I hope that next time
The team don't mess it up

READING BRAILLE

SW

I sail my fingerships
Over a paper sea
I do not see

I sail my fingerships
Across a dotted alphabet
Shaped like wave caps

Forward and back
I do not stop
Until I touch bottom

Of the great, wide page.

QUEEN OF TRAMPOLINE

SW

My friend Jeannie is the queen of trampoline.
She makes the most astounding bounds
    that I have ever seen.
Her triple-tuck-and-turnabout is flawless,
    and her form
When mounting and dismounting is a
    step above the norm.

My good friend Jeannie has an acrobatic gift,
Her ups and downs more forceful than a
    super-powered lift.
With death-defying circus tricks
    worthy of Houdini,
There's no kid on the trampoline
    as lean-and-mean as Jeannie.

I WISH I'D WRITTEN IT DOWN

RS

My mind was buzzing with ideas
the characters were crazy
Bill the bashful banjo player
Eloise and Maisie
The story was unfolding
As the scary, white-faced clown...
Then teacher said, Share with the class
But I didn't write it down

So, I can't remember what Bill said
When Maisie hid his shoes
Why the clown broke Billy's banjo
Or why Bill sings the blues

It isn't every day
That a meteorite hits town
Did Eloise escape or not?
I didn't write it down!

And so, the class are out to play
The sun is in the sky
I'm trying to think why Maisie winked
And what made Eloise cry

My pen is poised and ready
Is it an adverb or a noun?
It's the one thing I'm not good at
How do you write it down?

MOOSE

SW

Toughest kid
in the seventh grade
was Paul Corr —
known as Moose —
who'd hit a girl with glasses
for her lunch ticket

We feared him,
but I saw him once
running late
to a car
and a fat fist cuffed his cheek —
gift of Papa Moose

MARCHING BAND WOES

SW

There's saxophone and sousaphone,
Glockenspiel and xylophone,
And I get stuck with slide trombone.

I want a woodwind — oboe, flute,
Or better yet, a clarinet —
But slide trombone is what I get.

Some play tuba, cornet, trumpet,
Big bass drum so they can thump it.
Slide trombone? I'd rather dump it.

You say, "Haven't you even tried?"
I'll tell you, though it hurts my pride:
My arms are much too short to slide.

SCHOOL POND

RS

A scummy ballet
a broken chair
abandoned nets
weeds everywhere

A glimpse of frog
water trickling
slippery decking
accident waiting

SKATING LESSONS

SW

Tall,
Small,
We all
Fall
Once or
Twice.
Ice won't
Keep us
Upright
Long.
Is it wrong
To stop
And lend
A hand
To those
Who skate
And slide
And flop
And bravely
Stand?

ALONE IN THE CLASSROOM

RS

Crawling across the classroom
Is a black shiny beetle called Bill

A fat, furry fly called Fred
Sits on the window sill

A thin, hairy spider called Sid
Climbs up the classroom wall

A boy who's been naughty called Me
Sits on his own in the hall.

I am staying in at playtime
Just me, myself and I

All alone with my regrets
And a beetle, a spider, a fly

ERRAND FOR BILLY

RS

Run an errand for me, Billy
To the caretaker, Miss Wicks
I've run right out of sky hooks
I'll be needing twenty-six

Run an errand for me, Billy
To the school cook Mrs Wise
I need some milk and potatoes
To make the tees and dot the eyes

Run an errand for me, Billy
To the Head teacher, Miss Bun
And ask her if she has
A left-handed staple gun

Run an errand for me, Billy
If you would be so kind
And while you're gone we'll do some work
Hurry up and take your time

WHERE ARE MY MANNERS?

SW

On a pond's bottom
Trapped by a
Hippopotamus's
Knees
Lie my
May I
Thank You
Please
(Gesundheit
Bless You
When you
Sneeze)
And when I do
Recover these
You'll have my
Apologies.

LOST MY HOMEWORK

SW

No ravenous dog.

No Martian invasion.

No thirty-mile slog

To a family occasion.

No sudden swine flu.

No astronaut visit.

I'd homework to do.

You wonder, "Where is it?"

No grandmother died.

No nibbled by mouses.

No night trapped inside

The most haunted of houses.

No transformer crashed

Blacking out my whole block.

No asteroid smashed

Shelling me such a shock

That the part of my head

Where I store my assignments

Was tattered to shreds

And knocked out of alignment.

No bully's reprisal.

No baby bro's vomit.

No search of the skies

For a hundred-year comet.

No freak springtime snow.

No lottery winnings.

No open bus window.

No game past nine innings.

You say, "Give it here.

No lies. No excuses."

Is this the cold fear

That lost homework induces?

LAUGHTER, AND WHAT CAME AFTER

SW

The buzzard's beak of Mrs Bleak,

Our vulturous librarian,

Said, "If you rudely carry on

I'll turn you into carrion."

A dry gulch was her reading room.

Her desk, a mess of desert brush.

I tried to hide, but fell to dust

Beneath her all-consuming

HUSH!

THE END OF THE WORLD

RS

The world will end today
I heard it in the playground
Sam told Jake and Jake told Dee
And she told Ali and he told me
That it was on TV
The world will end today
Just ten minutes left to play
A lump of granite
Will hit the planet
And we'll be blown away
The world will end today
Ten seconds left — goodbye
I have to say
I'm feeling scared
'Cos I don't want to die.
The world will end today
It's ending right now as I speak
But look at the sky!
It's as blue as before
Maybe the world ends next week?

LIBRARY

(for Pilbright Library)
RS

I always thought
It would be cool
To run the library
In my school
I'd get to choose
From books galore
I'd read them all
And then buy more
Books of fact
Books of fiction
Dictionaries
And detection
Books of real-life
Baffling mysteries
Dinosaurs
And ancient histories
Harry Potter, obviously
And lots and lots
Of poetry
Rosen, Patten

And McGough
Adrian Mitchell
(I like his stuff)
Iron men and friendly giants
Books of chemistry and science
Angels in unlikely places
Duels fought
From fifteen paces
Long books, short books
Fat and thin
Where the good guys always win
Surely you agree with me?
All schools need a library.
A library in every town?
We must build more.
Not close them down.
For there's no better place to be
Than sitting in a library.

NASTY CHARACTERS

SW

Look —
If I had to be
Locked in a book,
I'd like to be trapped
With that crook Cap'n
Hook.

Heroes —
They're boring.
I find myself snoring
Or downright
Ignoring those
Zeroes.

In short,
If a plotter
Gives me Harry Potter,
I'd rather resort
To Lord Vol-de-
Mort.

Best,
In a pinch,
Is the Grinch
Or the Wickedest
Witch of the
West.

Still,
Stick me in a tale,
Like Jonah in a Whale.
I'm Jack — and my Jill
Is Cruella de
Vil!

MONSTER OF THE DEEP END

SW

Panic at the Public Pool —
Swimmers, come out of the water.
I'm the Creature from the Black Lagoon.
I am the Kraken's Daughter.

My head's got squiddy tentacles,
My tail's a flailing snake,
And I'm taking my vacation in
This chlorinated lake!

WE'RE HAVING A QUIET

RS

The class as usual is noisy
An uproar is well underway
Mr Walton comes in, looking upset and thin
And over the din says, Okay!
I've been up all night with my budgie
His plumage was pallid and grey
So I'm asking you all, please, not too loud.
We're having a quiet day.

We're having a quiet day.
We're having a quiet day.
We're having a quiet day.

Then the head pops her head round
    the classroom door
I've something to ask, if I may.
My daughter has brought her baby in
(There's another one on the way)
She's fast asleep in her little cot
And she looks so lovely and gay.
Let her sleep. Let her snooze.

Don't give her the blues.

We're having a quiet day.

We're having a quiet day.

We're having a quiet day.

We're having a quiet day.

A clearing of throat from the back of the room

It's the teaching assistant Miss Bray

She says, Five little sparrows have hatched in the nest

The one that their mum built last May

Let's be calm, let's not fuss

Let's whisper, let's hush

Be as quiet as the sunset's last ray

We mustn't disturb

Those dear lickle birds

We're having a quiet day

We're having a quiet day.

We're having a quiet day.

We're having a quiet day.

Now the classroom's as quiet as a dandelion clock,

As quiet as a knot's silent K

As quiet as a snowflake drifting down

From a windless sky of grey

Mr Walton is smiling, it's so satisfying

Like a favourite action replay

For nobody's shirking

The class are all working

We're having a quiet...

(Not having a riot)

We're having a really quiet day.

We're having a quiet day.

We're having a quiet day.

We're having a really quiet day.

CLUMSY

SW

We all stood up in the boat,
but I was the goat who fell out.
It's here in the photograph.
Jeremy holds the oar.
Melanie laughs as my splash
crashes to her knees.
Even the trees on shore
double over. (What a klutz!
What a bumbler!) I'm always
the stumbler, always the goof
whose shoelaces tangle.
(Have a nice trip!) No matter
the angle, I'll miss, I'll
mangle the free kick. I slip
and I fall. Some guys are born
graceful. Why do I get a face
full of dirt, a swim in the lake?
My mistake? I hope, when I'm
older, to sway and to
stay in the boat.

IF I WAS IN CHARGE

by RS (aged 10¾)

I'd say
Sit down!
Be quiet!
Take out your reading books.
Read silently!

I'd then
Peruse
My comic
And drink a cup
Of tea.

I'd pop up
To the staffroom
And eat a cake or three

Return, and say
Let's all go home
If it were up to me.

Let's open at ten
And close at one
A three-hour day's long enough

That's an hour for play
And hour for lunch
And an hour for learning stuff

HAIKU

RS

Mums at the school gate
Starlings in the autumn sky
Heading home to roost

HOME
TIMES

IT'S NOT MY FAULT

SW

My name is Walt.
It's not my fault.
My parents had their pick.

It's not my fault
I don't like salt.
It's gross and makes me sick.

I can't pole vault.
It's not my fault.
I'm not the one to blame.

It's not my fault
They call me Walt.
My parents chose the name.

IT WASN'T ME

RS

I didn't hide a spider inside of Sally's shoes
or draw a smiley face on my snoozing
    grandpa's head

I didn't tie together Terry's laces, or make faces
behind his back, or sneak a snail into my
    sister's bed
I didn't ride Mike's bike and leave it out when
    it was raining
I didn't bunk off school and go off to the
    pool instead
Don't be so judgemental, it's just coincidental
that my face has turned a shade of
    cherry red

SEVEN HORSES

SW

I have seven horses.

They live in my room.

There's Whiplash

And Scurvy

And Captain Kaboom.

There's Earthquake

And Toothache

And Double-Dog-Dare.

The seventh's a nag named

My Own Worst Nightmare.

I have seven horses

And sources of noise.

They unmake my bed

And they scatter my toys.

Mum's on the warpath.

Dad's talking Doom.

I have seven horses.

They live in my room.

WRITER

RS

I wrote the words
that made you sad
that made you sing the blues
But don't blame me
for feeling bad
I'm just the pen you use

BUBBLE

SW

I've blown a gum bubble as big as my brain,
And though I'm enormously proud,
I bet my poor ears that a brain bubble burst
Is intense and exceedingly loud.

I've blown a gum bubble as big as my brain,
And now I don't know what to do.
Do I let it aloft, like a Zeppelin to Spain,
Or chew like a ewe from Peru?

HAND CAUGHT IN THE COOKIE JAR

SW

Hand caught in the cookie jar,
What a naughty hand you are.
High above the shelf you slip
Swiping bites of chocolate chip.

If the cookie jar won't budge,
Or you've left a guilty smudge,
My advice is, just act dumb
When you're nabbed by Dad or Mum.

HELP AVAILABLE

RS

If you're feeling vexed
Send me a text
If you've got the glums
Ring up your chums
If you're feeling blue
Make a phone call or two
If you're not feeling great
Call up a mate
Want the blues to end?
Chat with a friend
Too much to take?
Then we'll go down to the beach and have a yummy
   ice cream with a chocolate
Flake

COWS

RS

There's a cow in the chemist, a cow in the baker's
A cow in the greengrocer's too
And when our short-sighted Gran said, excuse me young man
The young man turned round and said, MOO!
At the bus stop there was quite a palaver
'Cos a bus isn't made for a cow
And the bull had gone into the china shop
Which was not unexpected somehow
Well, this morning I took the shortcut through the fields
As I ran down the hill into school
It said Shut the Gate, but I was ten minutes late
I shut it most days as a rule

ODD ONE OUT

SW

Father sings, a cathedral bell.
Mother's operatic.
Sister solos in Giselle.
Me? — I'm problematic.

Half a year of playing harp
Then a harpsichord.
Flattened every major sharp.
Left each teacher bored.

Virtuoso at keeping silent.
Masterfully mum.
Even in the shower I
Don't so much as hum.

BYE BYE BILLY

RS

Billy left my bedroom in a mess
Billy hid the front door key
Billy posted Mum's credit cards through the
floorboards in the hall
Billy ate the last jam doughnut
Billy broke the window with his ball
Billy forgot to turn off the hot tap
Billy put the marbles in Grandpa's shoe
Billy broke Dad's ruler seeing how far it would bend

But now I'm twelve and Billy's gone
I'll miss my imaginary friend

EVIL TWIN

SW

It wasn't me — or was it He,
My evil, evil, evil twin?
I didn't mean to be so mean.
There goes my evil twin again.
He's never mild and always wild.
Thank goodness I'm an only child.

I'M SORRY

RS

As I lie here in bed
These words chase round my head
I'm sorry

Our head teacher said
That words can't be unsaid
I'm sorry
I called you scraggy bones
I called you maggot pie
I'm sorry
And when you cried, I laughed
I said, I hope you die
I'm sorry
I've been awake for hours
Tomorrow I will try to say
I'm sorry

MEDUSA

SW

Gorgon
Harpy
Ogress
Shrew

What if
those
applied
to you?

Fury
Hag
Temptress
Crone

Surely
you've got
a few snakes
of your own?

CASUALTIES OF WAR

RS

Tom and Tim
were best of friends
from the time that they could crawl
until Tom broke
Tim's Action Man
and Tim went up the wall.
From that day on
they never talked,
they never played a game
They grew up strangers
Don't you think
that really is a shame?

I'M LATE!

SW

I'm nearly always running late,
I'm rarely early for a date,
I totally procrastinate,

I'm tardy, slow, I've missed the boat,
I never swim when I can float,
My whereabouts are all remote,

I'm trapped, I'm strapped, delayer, waiter,
I'm slugabed, alarm-clock hater,
See You Later, Alligator...

I'm overdue, prompt's not my style,
Eleventh-hour on the dial,
In a While, Crocodile...

QUIET, I'M ON THE PHONE

RS

Mum, I'm thirsty. I need a drink!

Quiet I'm on the phone

Mum! The kettle's boiling

Quiet I'm on the phone

Mum, the microwave is on the blink

Quiet I'm on the phone

Mum, the neighbour's calling

Quiet I'm on the phone

Mum, a policeman's at the door

Quiet I'm on the phone

Mum, an alien's on the lawn

Quiet I'm on the phone

He's says he's from another galaxy

And he brings humankind love

And everlasting peace

Quiet I'm on the phone

Mum, I'm going! I'm leaving home.

There's some milkshake in the fridge

Thanks, Mum

Now be quiet, I'm on the phone

MY MOTHER'S GARDEN

SW

My mother's garden's overgrown,
A narrow plot of weed and stone.

She used to plant begonias there
And tended each new bulb with care.

But since she now works miles away
She's left her plot in disarray.

My brother and I are going to try
To grow new sunflowers three feet high.

GRANDAD'S PLANTS

RS

Grandad
Loved plants
He took hundreds of photos
Of plants
And mounted them in his album

And he would print out
Their names
On his computer
For the captions
Under the photographs

Rolling the words
Around his mouth
As if he were saying
A prayer

Santoline
Screwpine
Spearmint
Soapwort

Spikenard
Stonecrop
Sweetgale
Spearwort

SECRET WORLD

RS

You need a passport
To visit my secret world
Which you send for on the internet
Or you can get special permission
To make your own
As long as I stamp it
With my special intricate gold stamp
Most people fly there
Or go by time machine
But you can walk
If you know the secret way

I stumbled upon it walking Kenny, our dog
There was a gap
Where bits of the world
Don't quite join up
Like that shirt my gran made
And Kenny found it
Looking for a rat and I followed him

The weather?
Very hot and sunny all the time.
Although I went in winter once
And it rained nonstop
When I got home
I told Mum I'd fallen in the pond

I could take you there if you like.
To my secret world
If we went now
We'd be back in time for lunch

FLU SHOT BLUES

SW

I try NOT to get shots in my arm for the flu,
And it's not that I'm fraught with the harm
  it might do.

It's the pain — like a burr in the paw of a bear —
Oh the ache is a boa constrictor I wear.

When the snaky quick prick of its fangs
    nicks my skin
With its venomous, poisonous pinch, I begin

To unravel myself in a serpentine squeam
And I hiss like an asp, though I'd much
    rather scream.

But the part that annoys me the most is the sad
Mocking voice of my doc: "Was that really so bad?"

MAD SCIENTIST

SW

I'm perfectly sane... just a little upset.
My lab bench is smothered by smog.

I never was fond of the neighbour's cat,
But I might need to get a new dog.

CONVINCING MUM
WE NEED A DOG

RS

Please, Mum, let me have a dog.

No way!

I'll walk him every day.

So you say.

I'll get a job and buy all his food.

Get real!

He'll guard the house.

There's nothing here to steal.

Could I have a Gameboy, then?

You know we haven't got the money.

He'll help me with my homework.

Ha ha! Very funny.

He'll be company for you.

And cheer you up if you feel sad.

Well... I suppose that's true...

Can we have a dog then?

You'll have to ask your dad!

PELICAN

SW

If I can't get a dog then I guess I'll get a pelican.
A pelican I'll get if I can't get a dog.
Instead of a stick, I'll toss bright fish right
    into his pouch.
Instead of a walk, he'll wing like a kite on the
    string of his leash.
And late at night he'll settle his pelican head at the
    foot of my bed
Dreaming halibut dreams swimming up from
    the dark sea.

SISTER SAL'S SO GOOD WITH PEOPLE

RS

Sister Sal's so good with people
Knows the right things to say
Sister Sal can tell why
There's a cloud in the sky
She can see if it's silver or grey

Sal can see if Aunt Annie is angry
She can tell if Aunt Sadie is sad
And she knows to keep clear
When a storm's coming near
'Cos our Terry has upset our dad

On life's uncertain ocean I see only ships
And sailors at work on the decks
But Sal can make out
The way fish swim about
She sees enemy subs and old wrecks.

Yes, Sal can see under the surface
She can just understand so much more
Mum says this condition
Is called intuition
It's a dead useful trick, that's for sure.

COUSINS

SW

When my cousins come to stay
My whole house shivers and shakes,
And neighbours down the road dismay
On hearing the sound an earthquake makes
In toppling a mighty tower.
(My cousins are just that brash
And, all together, have the power
To turn a sturdy house to ash.)
When my cousins come to stay
I need a secret space to hide,
And though I dearly love my cousins
I wish I wish they'd stay outside.

KISS AUNT SUE?

RS

What? Kiss Aunt Sue?
I'd rather be fed to the lions at the zoo!
I'd rather be stuck to the ceiling with glue
I'd rather be cooked in a cannibal's stew
Or be chased by a cheetah to far Timbuktu!
Or white-water raft in a leaky canoe
Or hold my breath till my face is blue!
Or be made to drink a pink pint of shampoo
Or be dipped on a stick into chocolate fondue
Or wait for a year and a day in a queue
Or be bounced on the bonce by a bush kangaroo
Or tackle a master black-belt at Kung Fu

What? You'll give me a pound if I do?
Of course, I'd love to kiss Aunt Sue.

HOW CAN I BE LONELY?

RS

We're a family of eleven
And nearly everyone wants to play
So how can I possibly be lonely?
I ask myself each day

Mum works in the City of London
And Dad is a football scout
But that still leaves eight (not counting me)
So there's always someone about

Our cats, Alpha and Beta
They like a bit of fun
Chasing birds in the straggly
     bean patch
Or shadows in the sun

And our goldfish Zap and Trevor
You'll never meet fish nicer
I can watch them swim round and
     round for hours
First one way then versa vicer

Harry the hamster's quite funny
With his death-defying tricks
And Judy, our dog, doesn't say very much
But she's brilliant at bringing back sticks.

You can chat with Peter, the budgie
He'll discuss football, the Villa or Man U
He can talk the hind legs off a python
He can talk till his face turns blue

We're a family of eleven
And nearly everyone wants to play
So how can I possibly be lonely?
I ask myself each day

Oh, I nearly forgot — that's only ten
I've not mentioned my very best mate
If ever, by chance, I do get lonely
I chat to the garden gate.

SNOW-GO

SW

New year, first snow —
But I can't go
Outside to play —
Must try another day —
Oh well, that's that —
I've lost my hat.

Could I wear my hood?
Mum says, "No good.
Gotta find your hat."
(Wonder where it's at!)
I've searched each nook —
No hat, third look.

I found my sled
Underneath my bed.
And my white kitten
Stole my right mitten.
Buttoned my snowsuit.
Laced up one boot.

No hat, no snow —
Mine's a no-show.
Bad luck, bare head.
Stuck inside instead.
Couldn't feel much glummer.
Six months till summer...

OUT AFTER BEDTIME

SW

Somebody caught me.
Somebody saw.
Somebody snitched
And summoned the Law.

You're in deep trouble,
Somebody said.
I'm nowhere near sleep,
But I've been sent to bed.

DIFFICULT TIMES

DINOSAURS

SW

No one knows why the dinosaurs died.
Some say they turned into birds.
While others insist they faded to mist.
It's a riddle without any words.

We may never know how humans will go.
Or whether we'll live on and on.
Our riddle's the same; there's no one to blame.
And the answer means nil till we're gone.

IT'S NOT MY FAULT

RS

It's not my fault
that the ice cap
is melting into the sea
and that polar bears
will have nowhere to live
I've not got a car
don't blame me
It's not my fault
that the rainforest
is being cut down, tree by tree
I don't eat burgers
or drink fizzy drinks
I'm not fooled by ads on TV
It's not my fault
bankers are greedy
It's not my fault people are poor
It's not my fault
people are homeless
don't lay that one at my door
Grownups say, well...
it's complicated!

But just how hard can it be?
To look after our planet?
To feed kids who've no food?
Whose fault is that?
Don't blame me

MY WORLD

SW

Lonely world,
Only world I've known,
Mother of sky, land, sea.

Warming world,
Storming whirlwind world,
How did you come to be?

Discarded world?
No... a bombarded world
Billions and billions of years.

Surviving world,
Ever a thriving world,
I bless you with laughter and tears.

AVALANCHE

SW

Hardpack buckles
Up from below.
Bare white knuckles

Jut through snow.
A yeti's paw
Begins to grow

Claw by claw.
And mountainside,
Softened by thaw,

Unearths a tide
For fractured slabs
Of snow to ride.

The monster grabs
At all in its path,
Heaves and jabs

With wintry wrath
Aspens bowed
In aftermath,

Leaving a shroud
Of powder cloud!

THE EARTH BLOWS HOT, THE EARTH BLOWS COLD

RS

Ninety million years ago
The Arctic was warm
Imagine that

A forest stretching down
To the shoreline
To the warm water of the Arctic Ocean

And scientists say
That one day
The Arctic will be warm again

But how soon?
How soon?
Well, judging by reports of global warming,

Too soon.

MOUNTAIN

SW

A mountain's in the middle of my street
Where yesterday the way was clear.
A massive mound near fifty feet.
What's a mountain doing here?

Morning joggers stop and goggle.
Neighbours stare from every door.
Nothing like this sort of boggle
Ever blocked my street before.

SAD ARCHITECT

SW

Because the tide's rising measure
Drowns the sloping sand bar,
Smoothing over flat beach stones,
Flooding for its awful hour,
I will not build my parapet,
I will not build my tower.

FOR WE ARE MAINLY WATER

RS

We are the dreams
Dreamt in the beginnings of time
In the dark oceans
Beyond the penetrations
Of sunlight
In the hot larval springs
The dreams of tubeworms
And small crawling things

The dreams of plankton, coral
Stretching far and wide
The dreams of sun jewels glittering
Upon the world's roof

The dreams of herring, angelfish and octopi
Of killer shark and ray
The dreams of porpoises and whales
Crashing through the ocean's surface
And singing to the sky

And in our dreams
Our distant cousins
Move quite slowly
Like images trapped in four-inch glass
Embedded in our DNA
A water memory

For we are mainly water
Our body and our soul

GREEN TURTLE

SW

One hundred years she learned to swim,
To slow her breath, and to exhale,
Not breaching like a pilot whale
On surfacing at ocean's rim,
But peeking out her bony beak
To taste a gulp of gusty air.

One hundred years to reach full size,
To earn each scar that scores her back,
Engravings from a shark attack,
To win the wisdom of her eyes.
What tales she'd tell if she could speak!
But I can only stand and stare.

ANCIENT COMPANIONS

RS

You glide, never hurtle, through the sea
You look like an old-fashioned spaceship
Or like Jules Verne's iron-plated submarine

Baulan Turtle, soon you will be made extinct
Like so many of your ocean companions
By water pollution
And human hunters, after your eggs and sweet flesh

You've lived in the sea
For one hundred and fifty million years
How fragile life can be

WHAT DIFFERENCE CAN IT MAKE?

RS

One little plastic bag
I threw into the lake
One little plastic bag
What difference can it make?

Ten little plastic bags
Floating down the tributary
Ten little plastic bags
That's not very many

A million plastic bags
Floating in the sea
Destroying the ecosystem
And all because of me

WHALE SHARK

SW

Now, it might make you tremble
to think that I resemble
a four-lane tunnel funnelled to my core,
but of the class I'm ranked in —
devourers of plankton —
a blue whale beats me fifty feet or more.

And as for tonnage, I'm prodigious
(in certain circles quite prestigious)
and you might see this only as a boon,
but a shark who's not malicious
may still be thought delicious
impaled upon a hunter's sharp harpoon.

My friend, I ask you never to forget:
A whale shark shouldn't end up in a net.
And so I beg you always to recall:
The biggest fish that swims can also fall.

SUMATRAN ORANGUTAN

SW

"Arboreal" you call me? This is true.
Each day I build my sleeping nest anew.

What can I say? I like a sturdy bed
And a pillow of leafy branches for my head.

My diet? Fresh-plucked figs I just adore.
You'd classify me as a frugivore.

But I also like a bite of bark for lunch
And crickets, ants, and termites by the bunch.

How do I move? I grab a hanging vine.
Walking's great, but swinging suits me fine.

Is it safe up here? Real danger's on the ground.
I've found that — Wait! — do you hear that
   buzzing sound?

It's like an angry honeybee's high drone.
A noise that gives me shivers to the bone.

I'd rather greet a tiger's killing claw
Than meet a logger's forest-felling saw.

PARROT

SW

Things with wings
Can't always fly
And some with legs
Can't walk

Having a beak
Might allow you to speak
But life is more
Than talk

CALL ME LUCKY

RS

My human's smashing
He's really kind
And he spends all his time with me
He's a real leader

I talk to other dogs
They get left alone
Neglected sometimes
But my human
He's with me all the time

He shares his food
And even sleeps with me
We have a special doorway
And I keep him warm at nights
I'm such a lucky dog

MY DOG DIGGER

SW

My dog Digger's
Dug and dug
Deeper than any
Burrowing bug

Deeper than tree roots
Deeper than bones
Deeper than neolithic stones

Down below mine shafts
Down below wells
Down where hot magma roils and swells

Far beneath Earth's crust
Far beneath core
Digging where no dog's dug before

My dog Digger's
Partly Pomeranian
She's quite the mixed breed
She's also Subterranean

BLACK RHINOCEROS

SW

Charge you? We choose to stand.
Patience is our gift.
Lift our double-horned heads.
Shake us; we won't shift.
Let time, not poachers, budge us
Till the continents all drift.

BEARS REPEATING

SW

polar polar
(that's a bear)

panda panda
(isn't there)

grizzly grizzly
(she's no slouch)

koala koala
(has a pouch)

brown bear brown bear
(meets a black)

cinnamon
(and kodiak)

cave bear cave bear
(is extinct)

bears repeating
(don't you think?)

EARTH FAREWELL

RS

We say goodbye to Earth
From the moons of Jupiter
Some of us are weeping silently
Others are shouting angrily
As we climb aboard the last spaceship
Our work here is done

We rise like the final sunrise
Above a poisonous sea
Into the empty void of space
While far, far away, in another place
Like an old full-up skip
Around the sun
Limps the planet of our birth

MOVING TO ATLANTIS CITY, 2112

SW

Eleven billion side by side
Take up a lot of space.
We needed fresh solutions quick
To house the human race.
We first built floating towns as big
As islands on the sea.
But soon these grew too overstuffed
For Dad and Mum and me.
We'd watched a holo on the web:
New Lab Needs Volunteers!
Mum and Dad signed up to be
Among the pioneers.
Of all the kids they picked to live
Beneath the ocean's rim
I wasn't quite the perfect choice.
I couldn't even swim.
But once we rode the shuttle down
And passed the pressure sphere
I knew there was no surface place
So much like Home as here.

Although I sometimes miss the sun
And unrecycled air,
I'd never trade my deep dark view
With all of you up there.

NEW MOON RISING

RS

When the wind is wailing and shrieking
And high clouds swirl the sky
Shout a wish to the new moon rising
And at midnight you'll hear the reply

But be careful what you shout out
At the night and her magical crew
For a wish that is wished at the new moon
Has a habit of coming true.

Why not wish for a fairer planet
Is it really too much to expect?
That the people of Earth be kindly and wise
And will treat their home with respect?

NIGHT SONG

SW

I sing of night, of hunting cats and stars,
Night-dark fences, rimed birch branches,
Black-topped roads, headlamps, cars.

I sing of night, of campfires and owls,
Silkspun spider traps, dripping water taps,
Moonlit mushroom caps, hound howls.

I sing of night, of hoarfrost and dreams,
Goblin haunts and graveyard stones,
What is, and is not what it seems.

AURORA BOREALIS

SW

Over the shores of Labrador
a certain rippling purple curtain
scatters light throughout the night.
(Wait — the colour's now a duller
hue of violet-turning-blue!)
This Arctic veil, a breaching whale
could peer behind, and still be blind
as anyone. The northern sun
has bent to drape her gauzy cape
across the skies, and left my eyes
to stare and stare at the glittering air.

TREE HOUSE

SW

I don't like the sound
Of living on the ground.
Too heavy and slow, like a rhino, for me.
My personal ranch is
The uppermost branches
Of a flowering, finch-embowering tree.

I don't need a crane
To enter the plane
Of existence where altitude's right.
A blimp of a bat
Floats me to my flat
And, moon-high, I pass the night.

REFUGEE CAMP

SW

Mama held my hand
As we walked on small hills
Toward a border town.

Papa wore a frown.
The baby had the chills,
And this was foreign land.

Racket of hammers and drills
From shelters built on sand,
Tents of muddy brown.

Families stuck like stills
In a scrapbook. A crown
Of sun, a cold command.

So tired he couldn't stand,
Pa laid the baby down
To rest. He'd brought no pills

And wouldn't speak a noun
To a nurse in a Red Cross band
Who tried to judge our ills.

He whispered, "Understand:
It's not this war that kills,
But begging in a border town."

SNIPER

RS

Mum gives Tarik a hug
Don't cross the Square
It may be further via the church
But it's safe. You're not in open view.

And tell him, Belma sends her love
That might be worth an extra loaf or two
I know he has the flour still
And while you are there
Ask him, What news of Ivan?

Mum gives Tarik another hug
And whispers a short prayer
Go now, she says
And do not cross the Square.

IF ONLY

SW

If only trees stayed where they're planted.
If only birds knew how to fly.
If only a mouse was as small as a stone.
Or fish didn't drop from the sky.
If only the moon pulled the tides in.
Or telescopes stared into space.
If only my pocket did not hold the world.
If only there were such a place.

RELEASE

SW

All my worries,
purple sugar
maple leaves,

I give them up —
gymnasts on
autumn gusts

TO MOTHER EARTH

RS

The land is black
The seas are brown
I'm sorry
That we let you down

PRAYER

RS

Let me walk in the fields and the forest
In a land that is rich and fair
Let me swim in the cool, clean ocean
Let me breathe untainted air

Let the sun's rays warm my body
Let the sun's light into my soul
Let us pray for this damaged planet
That one day it will heal and be whole

NOW WRITE
YOUR OWN

NOW WRITE YOUR OWN!

We hope you've enjoyed these poems.
Now, why not have a go at writing
one yourself? Here are some ideas
to help you get started.

IT WASN'T ME

I didn't hide a spider inside Sally's shoes
or draw a smiley face on my snoozing
   grandpa's head
I didn't tie together Terry's laces, or make faces
behind his back, or sneak a snail into my
   sister's bed
I didn't ride Mike's bike and leave it out when
   it was raining
I didn't bunk off school and go off to the
   pool instead
Don't be so judgemental, it's just coincidental
that my face has turned a shade of
   cherry red

Anyone can write poetry. Here's how you write a poem like "It Wasn't Me".

First imagine who is telling the story. Invent a character. The 'I' in the poem isn't you. It's someone you've made up. My character is called Billy.

Make a list of your character's friends and family. My list consists of Sally, Grandpa, Terry, Billy's sister and Mike. You could add teachers, people your character plays sport with — anyone at all — to your list.

Now think of a trick you could play on each of those people and write it beside their name. Don't be violent or rude. Instead try to be clever and funny. Small scary animals or squashy things appearing in unexpected places are often amusing.

My list ended up like this:
Sally — spider in shoe
Grandpa — draw on bald head
Terry — tie shoelaces together
Sister — put snail in bed
Mike — ride his bike
School — bunk off

Now it's time to write your first draft.
Begin each line of the poem with 'I didn't'.
My first draft looked like this:

I didn't put a spider in Sally's shoe

I didn't draw on Grandpa's head when he was asleep

I didn't tie Terry's shoe laces together

I didn't put a snail in my sister's bed

I didn't ride Mike's bike and leave it out in the rain

And I didn't bunk off school to go swimming

I then worked on it to make it more interesting.
Look at the finished poem to see what I did. Don't try
and make it rhyme, or it might sound contrived. But
if there are some there by accident, then that's fine.
You could add some adjectives and some alliteration.
Next, think of a good ending. I decided that Billy's
face would go bright red.

Before you write your finished version, ask yourself — are all the tricks funny? Maybe leave out any that are boring or you've heard before. How about giving someone in the poem an unusual or funny name? Lastly, read the poem out loud, and listen. Does it have a nice rhythmic flow?

Good luck!

Roger Stevens

OUT AFTER BEDTIME

Somebody caught me.
Somebody saw.
Somebody snitched
And summoned the Law.
You're in deep trouble,
Somebody said.
I'm nowhere near sleep,
But I've been sent to bed.

One thing that can make a poem memorable is the skillful use of repetition. You can repeat anything in a poem: vowels, consonants, words, phrases, or even entire lines.

As with any other technique, too much repetition can become monotonous — the same note sounded again and again — so the writer (that's you!) needs to have a good ear for variation.

In my poem, I repeat "somebody" to create a simple pattern over three lines that I vary in the fourth line. I also repeat the "sum" sound in "summoned". Repeating the start of lines is called anaphora (uh-NAH-for-uh), and poets and public speakers use this tool often.

In the second group of lines (a stanza), I begin a new pattern but bring "somebody" back in line 2 as an echo to help connect the two stanzas.

Here's a way you can practise this type of repetition. Choose a subject and write a short poem that repeats the name of your subject. Keep it simple, and vary your last line as a small surprise for the reader. For example, in a poem about thunder:

Thunder grumbles.
Thunder roars.
Thunder stuns.
I stay indoors.

It's your turn. Your poem can be silly or more serious,
and it does not need to rhyme.

Have fun!

Steven Withrow

ACKNOWLEDGEMENTS

"How Can I Be Lonely" first appeared in
The Truth About Parents by Roger Stevens,
David Harmer, Brian Moses and Paul Cookson
(Macmillan Children's Books, 2009)

"Alone in the Classroom" first appeared in
On My Way to School I Saw a Dinosaur
by Roger Stevens (A & C Black, 2010)

"Prayer" first appeared in
Let's Recycle Grandad (A & C Black, 2008)

"Aurora Borealis" and "Avalanche"
first appeared in *The National Geographic Book
of Nature Poetry*, edited by J. Patrick Lewis
(National Geographic, 2015)

"Moving to Atlantis City, 2112"
first appeared in *The Poetry of Science:
The Poetry Friday Anthology for Science for
Kids*, compiled by Sylvia Vardell and Janet Wong
(Pomelo Books, 2015)

"Reading Braille" first appeared in
The Poetry Friday Anthology for Celebrations,
compiled by Sylvia Vardell and Janet Wong
(Pomelo Books, 2015)

"Green Turtle" first appeared in
The Poetry Friday Anthology,
compiled by Sylvia Vardell and Janet Wong
(Pomelo Books, 2012)

All are reproduced with the permission of the poets.

LIST OF POEMS

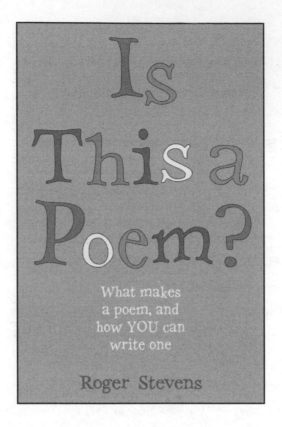

Is This a Poem?

What makes
a poem, and
how YOU can
write one

Roger Stevens

ISBN: 9781472920010

Do you like poems? Are you sure
you know what one is?!

This book is packed with every type of poem
you've ever heard of (and a few you haven't)!

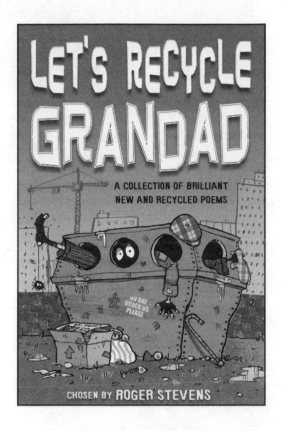

ISBN: 9780713688511

Another irresistible collection of brilliant poems
from Roger Stevens, to make you laugh,
cry, and feel green!

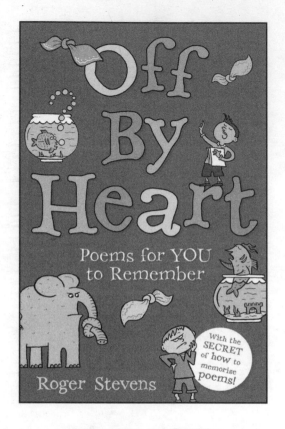

Off By Heart

Poems for YOU to Remember

With the SECRET of how to memorise poems!

Roger Stevens

ISBN: 9781408192948

A wonderful collection of poems full of rhythm and rhyme that are easy to learn by heart and perfect for reciting out loud.